Karissa Hampton

You Belong Here

Dedicated to my own little mermaid,

Layla.

A mermaid
named LAYLA
lives deep
in the clear,
blue ocean.

She loves to swim and play with her friends in the coral reef.

There are all sorts of beautiful fish and plants that live there too. They all belong to a delicate ecosystem.

One day Layla
notices a white
piece of paper
floating along
the surface of
the water.

Layla swims to the surface to collect the paper.

The next day, Layla finds a plastic bottle rocking along the waves of the water. "This does not belong here," she says.

Layla swims to the shore to find a recycle bin of plastic to place it in.

The next day Layla
is surprised to find
cardboard, aluminum
cans and plastic straws
littering her home.

Among the trash Layla notices a large net that must have been left behind by a fisherman passing by. Suddenly, Layla has a brilliant idea!

"I know how I can clean up our home," She says. Layla begins to tie the net to the end of her tail.

Layla begins to swim with all her might.

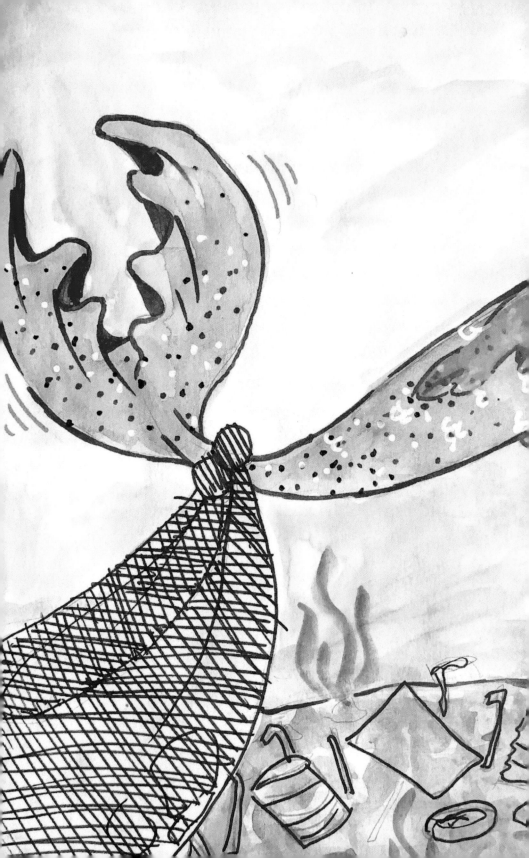

Layla swims and she swims until her tail is heavy with trash.

Next, Layla lifts the net all the way to the shore where she finds three bins of recycle.

"You belong here," she says as she places the cardboard in a bin for paper.

Layla smiles, for she knows that even though it isn't her trash, it is her responsibility to help take care of the ocean.

Layla then swims
back to her home
where she belongs.

THE END